My beautiful **BABA**

Have you seen him?

From left to right, my big sisters
ADELFA, FER & LUCY

LEILA
(That's me!)

To my favorite witch,
my sister, Paola

No animals or magical beings were
harmed during the making of this book.

First US edition 2022

Library of Congress Catalog Card Number 2021947909
ISBN 978-1-5362-2050-6 (English hardcover)
ISBN 978-1-5362-2538-9 (Spanish hardcover)

APS 27 26 25 24 23 22
10 9 8 7 6 5 4 3 2 1

Printed in Humen, Dongguan, China

This book was typeset in Copse.
The illustrations were done in mixed media.

Candlewick Press
99 Dover Street
Somerville, Massachusetts 02144

www.candlewick.com

CANDLEWICK PRESS

LEILA
THE PERFECT WITCH

And then Hansel and Gretel broke in and ate everything!

FLAVIA Z. DRAGO

Far and wide, Leila Wayward was known
for being an extraordinary little witch.

She lived with her baba and
three big sisters, Adelfa, Fer, and Lucy,
in their cozy gingerbread house.

She was always the fastest flier . . .

the most cunning conjurer,

the sneakiest shape-shifter,

and the craftiest carver
in her coven.

For each of her talents, Leila had won a trophy, but she was saving a special spot for the most important one of all.

SUMMONING SHAPESHIFTING ALCHEMY MAGIC APPLES

PUMPKIN CARVING FLYING HERBOLOGY

POTIONS SPELLING

After all, Leila was the youngest in a long line of powerful women who were experts in the Dark Arts of Patisserie.

And this year, she was
finally old enough to
enter the competition.

But much to Leila's surprise . . .

baking wasn't such
a piece of cake!

Of course, Leila wasn't going to give up.
*I want to be as good as everyone
in my family,* she thought.

Leeeilaaaaaa, wanna chase fairies and forage for mushrooms?

But if she wanted to win,

there would be no time to go out and fly,

no time for carving pumpkins,

and definitely no time for fun! Leila was, after all,
a particularly determined witch.

Finally, after a lot of research,
Leila found the perfect recipe.

And after a lot of experimenting and hard work, she was about to make the most magical . . .

But as it turned out . . .

good sisters will always be there,
especially when you need them the most.

Fer showed Leila her best tricks for sifting and mixing,

Lucy helped her whip the cream,

and Adelfa taught her everything about decoration techniques.

But, most importantly, they all had so much fun!

Finally, the night of the Magnificent Witchy Cake-Off had arrived. The judges and contestants were ready.

Leila put on her chef's uniform,
and off she went.

Little by little . . .

And try again!

she got there!

YOU ARE THE BEST WITCH

So in the end, Leila didn't win that trophy.

We are so proud of you!

But losing wasn't as terrible as she'd imagined it might be.
And you know what?

When she was having fun, she felt like a winner.

Plus, there was one thing that all the Waywards
would always be extraordinarily good at . . .

eating cake together!

MONSTER CAKE

INGREDIENTS:

~~Eye of newt~~

~~Toe of frog~~

Mandrake seeds

Nightshade

Wool of bat

Foul troll's flour

Slug bones

Devil's cherries

Unicorn farts

MIX